For Tony, with love
_ MCB

For Ella + Alan
_ TM

Text copyright © M. Christina Butler 2004
Illustrations copyright © Little Tiger Press 2004

Original edition published in English by Little Tiger Press, an imprint of Magi Publications, London, England, 2004.

Printed in China

Library of Congress Cataloging-in-Publication Data

Butler, M. Christina.
One snowy night / M. Christina Butler ; pictures by Tina Macnaughton.
  p. cm.
Summary: Awakened from hibernation when an ill-fitting, gift-wrapped red wool cap falls nearby, Little Hedgehog passes along the present to Rabbit, but somehow ends up with it again by the end of the day.
ISBN 1-56148-452-0 (hardcover)
[1. Hedgehogs--Fiction. 2. Animals--Fiction. 3. Christmas--Fiction. 4. Hats--Fiction.]   I. Macnaughton, Tina, ill. II. Title.
PZ7.B97738On 2004
[E]--dc22

2004027642

One Snowy Night

M. Christina Butler

Pictures by Tina Macnaughton

Intercourse, PA 17534
800/762-7171
www.goodbks.com

The cold wind woke Little Hedgehog
from his deep winter sleep. It blew his
blanket of leaves high into the air,
and he shivered in the snow. He tried
to sleep again, but he was much too cold.

Suddenly, something fell from the sky . . .

···THUD!

It landed right in front of his nose.
It was a present, and it had his name on it.

To Little Hedgehog
With Love From
Father Christmas xx

Little Hedgehog opened the present as fast as he could. Inside was a red wooly hat . . .
hedgehog size!

He put it on at once.
He pulled it to the back.
He pulled it to the front.
He pulled it to one side,
then the other . . .

But it didn't matter how he stretched it
to fit. His prickles got in the way *every time*.
By now the hat was much too big for a
little hedgehog.

He took it off and stared at it,
until at last he had an idea . . .

He gave the hat a shake
and wrapped it up again.
He ripped a piece off the
label and wrote on
the rest.

Then he ran to Rabbit's house.
Rabbit was out, so he left the present
on his doorstep.

It was snowing hard as
Little Hedgehog tried to find his
way back home. The snowflakes flew
all around, and he wasn't sure
which way to go.

"Oh dear, oh dear," he said as he
wandered to and fro. "I shouldn't have
come out in this weather. But I know
Rabbit will be happy to have a nice
wooly hat to wear."

"Too much snow!" said Rabbit, rushing home. He saw the present lying on his doorstep.

"What's this?" he squeaked with delight, ripping off the paper. "A wooly hat," he cried. "For ME!"

Happy Christmas Rabbit
With Love From
Little Hedgehog xx

He put it on at once. He tried it with
his ears inside, and then outside.
He pulled it this way and
he pulled it that way.
But it didn't matter how
he stretched it to fit.
His ears got in
the way . . .
every time.

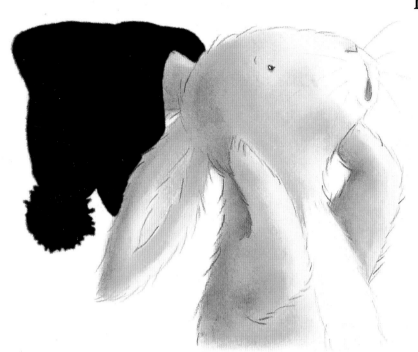

By now the hat was
much much bigger. It was
much too big for a rabbit.
So . . .

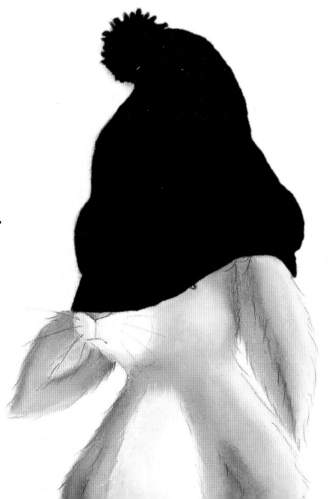

. . . Rabbit wrapped up the hat once again
and wrote on a corner of the label.
Then he went to visit Badger.

The cold weather made Badger very
grumpy.
  "Merry Christmas, Badger!"
shouted Rabbit.
  "Who's there?" growled Badger.
  "Merry Christmas!" repeated Rabbit,
giving him the present.

"A Christmas present?"
said Badger.
"For ME?"

Badger put the hat on.
He pulled it down over his ears.
 "How . . . about . . . THAT!"
he said, looking in the mirror.
 "Very nice," said Rabbit.
 "What did you say?" said Badger.
 "Very nice!" yelled Rabbit,
hopping off.

"Don't you like it?" asked
Badger, turning around.
But Rabbit had gone.
    Badger took the hat off.
"I can't use this hat,"
  he said. "I can't hear
  a thing. Too bad—it's such a
  nice color."

So Badger wrapped up
the present and marched
off to Fox's house.
He didn't use
a label.

Fox was going out exploring.

"Here you are, friend," said Badger merrily.

"A Christmas present, just for you!"

"Christmas?" snapped Fox, puzzled.

"Yes, Christmas!" called Badger.

"Time to be nice to each other!"

And he trudged home.

"A hat?" sneered Fox, opening the present. "Why would I want a hat?"

Then he looked at the hat again . . .

He made two holes for his ears and put it on. Satisfied, he went on his way.

The white fields twinkled in the
moonlight. Fox sniffed around and
found a small trail. He followed it this way
and that way until suddenly it stopped.
There was something under the snow!

Fox dug and dug,
until he found a small hedgehog.
It was cold and did not move.
"Poor little guy," said Fox.
He put the hedgehog inside the
red wooly hat and carried
it to Rabbit's house.

Rabbit and Badger were having supper.
"Look what I've found in the snow!"
cried Fox, bursting in.
They all looked into
the hat.

"A hedgehog?" said Badger.
"What's a hedgehog doing out at
Christmas time? He should be fast asleep!"
"It's my friend Little Hedgehog!" cried
Rabbit. "He must have gotten lost going
home in the snow!"
Little Hedgehog opened his eyes.
"Hello," he said sleepily. "Oh, this
is such a lovely warm blanket."

The friends all looked at each other.
Rabbit grinned and Fox scratched his head.
"Hmmm," said Badger. "I think this wooly
hat is *just right* for Little Hedgehog!"
"Merry Christmas, Little Hedgehog!"
they all cried . . . but Little Hedgehog
was fast asleep.